Incoming

S.J James

Incoming.

Contents

The Game

It began with a game, as all things do.

We were twelve, playing in the attic, heroes armed in our finest gear: cushions, taped around our middle, sunglasses sat askew atop our heads; beach towels tied around our necks with rubber bands found on streets pooled around our wrists, broom handles and mop sticks in our hands.

Harrison was on watch duty, perched up by the window. He was the youngest, the smallest, so his legs folded with ease onto the windowsill. His hands lay pressed against the glass, green eyes vigilant, darting about as our battle raged on behind him.

What a sight we must have made.

Five pairs of scrawny limbs flailing about a dimly lit room, lashing out at nothing with the gusto of past kings and conquerors that we learnt of in classrooms.

Xzalia was the eldest, the first to reach thirteen and thus she was the commander, giving us our orders. On her call, we marched, at her whistle we charged, capes trailing behind us as we swung and speared at shadows and empty spaces.

"5 o'clock!"

"Watch your left!"

"Again!"

"Strike!"

"Charge!"

"Incoming!" came Harrison's call.

We halted mid-battle and awaited the sound of crunching gravel, the familiar 'putt-putting' of Matthieu's mother returning, the hum-drum droning of his brothers as they raced for the living room tv. There came nothing but silence. Still, we froze, awaiting

Harrison's go ahead, reluctant at the thought of our war continuing another day.

"Clear!"

On we went through the day, battling forces only we could see.

We'd gathered provisions early in the morning , anticipating a long war when the day's battleground was chosen. We scarfed down hastily buttered rolls and munched on cheese slices in between bouts of manic movements, thick dough softened by soured lemonade and bitter apple juice.

We learnt to take slow sips and not gulped mouthfuls after Dennis spent several minutes in the corner spluttering as Matthieu pounded on his back.

"Don't down it in one go, idiot," he snorted as Dennis wiped errant tears from his cheeks. "If you die, we can't play anymore."

"It tastes like piss."

"Mum says it's organic."

"Let's move!" Xzalia called out, and we all rushed back into action, mops flailing in the air as we attacked frozen dust bunnies and moth eaten curtains hanging from the ceiling that seemingly danced away from us.

"Wait!" cried Harrison, having never left his post. His face pressed into the glass, leaving faint puffs of air against the window that dissipated in seconds. We froze yet again, ears straining.

"What did you see?" I asked him under hushed breath. At his continued silence, I glanced up and caught sight of his eyes in the window reflection, his pupils blown, fixed on the grey landscape outside.

"Harrison?" Dennis broke from formation to peek out beside Harrison. "No one's there."

Then came the sound of the doorbell.

It was an ancient thing, befitting the house, rusted wiring connecting it to the pulley by the front door. It was so old, the sound it made came as a low groan, rising steadily in volume until it was bellowing by the last of

the three pulls needed to work it.
The bell itself hung above the living room
mantlepiece, a large intimidating remnant of
a bygone era, that required a professional
with an exceptionally long step-ladder just
to dust it, let alone tune it.

It was for this reason Mrs. Walburgess
forbade anyone from touching it.

There came the sound again, agitated, as if
the bell itself were calling out to us for help.
I felt a decided shift in the air, as
goosebumps began to rise on my arms, our
imagined threats suddenly made very real.
We were alone, and the visitor insistent.

It crept on us, a silent understanding,
suddenly aware of the noise we had been
making. It rang one more, warbling with
tremendous strain, and at the nod from
Xzalia, we called out our pledge of
allegiance in unison, drowning out the
dying strains:

LEE LI LO LAH

TEN ARMS

TEN EYES

FIGHT FOR ONE

AS ONE UNITE

Fists in the air, we rejoiced at the answering crunch of retreating boots.

Like the foolish infants we were, we cheered, declared it a victory and delighted in what we mistook as an act of surrender.

In all the excitement, Harrison looked away from his post.

And that was when the monsters struck.

Set

No one believed us when we told them.

They said we were in shock, denial – "a guilty conscience can create the greatest of *delusions*-"

But we weren't guilty. And they weren't delusions.

Shadows bore witness as limbs squelched under strain, eyes bulging, terrifyingly clear.
His curdling wails of terror ring just as clear as they first did so many years ago.
His blood a bitter coppery film that coated my mouth, my throat, and choked me in the early hours of night; the rusted smell that

followed me around, the feel of petrified flesh giving way-

No. Not delusions.

We made frontpage news across the country, and the better half of the continent. Several months passed as we awaited the verdict, the dust attempting to settle around us disrupted with every article feature, lingering camera and concealed microphone.

Then came the call- we were to be separated, have our parents send us away.

Words like 'rehabilitation' and 'deportation' shrouded us as we were sent away, but as time crept by, they were followed by reports of 'exile' and 'isolation'.

That night saw Dennis returned to his father in Grenada, a man he'd only heard of; his aunt refused to spare him even a glance as he was taken away, her disgust immortalised in the paper the next day.

Xzalia was branded the ringleader and carted to South Africa with her parents under a cloud of hushed whispers, leaving behind a racial storm that continued in the her absence.

Matthieu's family abandoned the house entirely, refusing to sell it to the growing cult of fanatics that emerged as if from the echoes of the grounds themselves.
They absconded in the night, returning to their Parisian home and maiden name, where the words 'Walburgess murder house' were left to haunt the young boys at Father John's Guided Academy- a remote boarding school on the other side of the country- when a shivering Matthieu joined their ranks.

The matter of guardianship was left with an estranged uncle, a veteran by the name of Rosco, of whom there was no trace.

There was nowhere for my mother to hide, nor tuck me away from the whispers and vultures that circled our home. By the time they came for me, I lay beside her broken body, rendered un-recognisable by time, yet still I held on and cried.

*

I was brought to a group home by the sea.

It was my first time travelling so far, the train sights blurring into one as it began to rain.

"You'll get used to it," the social worker told me as we left the idyllic fields of green and familiar buildings behind us. Chalky greys and whites surrounded us, enclosing us against the grey restlessness of the ocean. I'd never seen the sea before.

When we arrived, it quickly became clear the news had reached even this sleepy costal town. They were all afraid of me; the six children shied away and the parents- Laura and Dean- grew wary at the sight of me. I caught snippets of their hushed conversation one morning as I waited for the sun to crest over the dim horizon.

I couldn't sleep most nights.

"- you say yes? Of all the cases-"

"-just a boy-"

"- little monster! Think of the kids-"

"-can manage, just a month or two-"

The floorboards creaked and their voices faded away as they moved down the stairs. I kept my gaze on the sun as dawn broke, casting an amber glow on the walls and window.

We went down to the beach one Sunday just after church. It had been a little over two months since I'd arrived, yet this was the first time I accompanied them to the little stone church by the pier. Sundays were usually reserved for my weekly check-in with the social worker, only it had been a while since she'd last visited. The last two weeks I had spent alone, seated at the corner booth in the village café, nibbling on buttered toast gone cold, bought and ignored by Dean, who left as soon as could be.

I was seated at the far back, alone on the pew; Laura claimed the other children needed an adult with them at the front, and Dean refused to sit near me in church, leaving the room halfway through prayers.

He said he needed some fresh air, but I knew.

The pastor was an old man in his middling fifties who cast a stern eye over me as he rambled down the psalm of forgiveness. At my stuttered responses, he turned away from me with a firm 'harrumph'. I tuned my thoughts towards the chilling spray of the fierce ocean waves just outside.

As the younger children ran about on the sand, I followed the older boys and girls into the nearby caves.

Hanna and Elsie wanted me to leave, but John and Peter grew brave and resisted. There was only one of me after all. I could have told them about the monsters, whose presence I felt keenly even then, but I only wanted a friend. Someone to play heroes with. So I said nothing and went along with their games.
I ran, roared and said whatever they wanted to hear. When they grew bored, Peter and Elsie wandered off together, and John went to follow them with his camera. He ordered me to stay behind and watch Hanna, , whose honey brown skin had rapidly gone grey as

the day progressed. Ever the obedient soldier, I took his place beside her as he lumbered off.

We sat in silence, looking off into the direction they'd taken.

"Did you really eat him?"

I looked at her, but her eyes were fixed on the cave entrance, her teeth worrying away at her lip.

"No."

"So how did he die?"

I wrestled with myself. Do I tell her the truth? Would she even believe me if I did?

She still wouldn't look my way.

"It was the monsters." She shivered, and faced towards me, her eyes on the ground.

"Why didn't they kill the rest of you?"

I wanted to cry. How many nights had I asked myself that same question? Sat by the window, waiting to hear the familiar groan that had marked their arrival, stood rigid as I

sensed the same charge in the air that had
enveloped us all in Matthieu's attic that day.
The answer remained ever steadfast.

"I don't know."

*

Eventually, they grew discontent in their
passivity; the monsters would claim another
of us.

When we were separated, Xzalia's parents
claimed they needed to go back home, to
their roots and figure things out. The return
to culture would do her some good, they
claimed. On the third month of my stay, I
received a letter from Dennis, a torn
newspaper article folded inside, and a scrap
of paper with a hastily scrawled message:

they're going to eat us too

I unfolded the article with shaking hands.

'CANNIBAL CHILD KILLED BY
CARNIVORE IN FREAK ACCIDENT.'

Mr and Mrs Naidoo returned without their
daughter, claiming they'd gotten separated
during a safari, and a lion had eaten her.
Only her bloodied shoes were found at the
scene, a described bloodbath at the scene.

I spent that night curled up under my bed, a
chair underneath my door. Laura came to
check on me, somewhat begrudgingly and
at my silence, sent up first Dean

　　　　"Listen you little demon, if you
don't come out of there-"

then Peter

　　　　"Hey Canni, get out here, one of
your chow pals got eaten, it's like the
ultimate karma-"

and even Hanna

　　　　"-It's me. I hear about your friend,
and I- I just want you to know I'm here if
you want to talk. It's just you and me."

I did want to talk. I wanted to crawl into my mother's arms and have her tell me none of this was my fault, and that everything would be okay. But I couldn't open the door couldn't look away from the shadows dancing over the window's surface.

The monsters were waiting to come in.

Matched

I wrote to Dennis twice, but I didn't hear from him again.

The last month I spent at the home, a change had taken place. The tenuous peace frayed and gave way to arguments, fights, separation.

I became Peter's favourite trick - he only had to bring me into the room, and the little ones would clam up and watch me with wide eyes as Peter waxed on about all the children I had eaten before, Elsie squealing just as loudly as the others.
When the tales grew too gruesome, one of

the little boys began carrying a paring knife in his pocket. A few days later, my carer came to take the little ones away, sparing me but a glance as she walked them out.

Laura didn't handle the change very well, and it began to show in the half-thawed lasagnas and stray bones and shelling littered in the one-dish fish pies.

Elsie fell pregnant and neither John nor Peter came forward as the father. John stopped coming home altogether, and Peter soon followed. Elsie was often heard throwing up at intervals throughout the day, before flitting in and out of the house for hours at a time.

Laura handled this about as graciously as she had everything else; she no longer left her room except for food and the occasional tormented glance she threw my way on the days I spent indoors. Dean buried himself in his work, staying out later and later, appearing early in the mornings and leaving scant hours later.

Hanna was the exception. Hanna stayed.

I showed her how to play heroes and we spent hours in the caves at the beach, fighting off monster invasions with swords and plasma rays, training for the day we'd need to turn our fight towards the intruders.

"They're coming in from everywhere! Look, over there-"

"Keep your eyes on your post Harrison!"

A beat of silence.

"Sorry- I-I meant-"

"It's okay-"

"-Hanna-"

"I know."

Another beat.

"We should take a quick break."

"Do you miss him?"

"…yes."

"…I miss my mum."

A sniffle.

"…me too."

A rustle.

"Come here."

*

It is said that air is still in the seconds before lightning strikes.

That last week, a storm was brewing somewhere in the Atlantic. The sea became unpredictable, and we found ourselves locked in the house for the first time in weeks, with Laura and Dean absent. We were seated in the living room as I flicked between the channels. Hanna sat by the window, looking out at tempest beyond.

Keeping watch.

Elsie flounced in, carrying with her a gust of cool salty air and the scent of midsummer rain. Her blond hair fell in drenched ringlets dripped down her face as she shed her coat and gingerly lowered herself to the sofa. She had just begun to show, a slender curve appearing through the damp fabric. Her dark eyes caught mine in the tv reflection, and she hastily tugged a nearby throw over her abdomen.

"What are you staring at?" she asked with a pinched frown.

I turned away, resuming my idle flicking through the channels. There was a startling flash from outside, accompanied by a thunderous clash and the television screen cut to black for a moment.

I cannot say when exactly I felt the shift.

Perhaps it was when I took notice of just how small and slight Hanna seemed in that instant, reflected in the black mirror of the screen, pressed up against the glass, her clear hazel eyes fixed on the darkening horizon. I distantly registered the tv screen flickering on.

27

I wanted to call out to her, but my tongue felt heavy, saliva rapidly pooling in my mouth as the faint strains of a guttural cry seemed to echo around me.

"…are urged to keep an eye out for a young boy believed to have run away from the Academy earlier this evening. The boy, 'Matthieu Walburgess 'is categorised as 'potentially dangerous.' If sighted-"

My head snapped towards the screen.

Matthieu's horror-stricken eyes seared into mine, alongside that of another. Pale faced, wide eyed, with tufts of hair sprouting in all directions. He looked like Harrison.

"... are still trying to find the remains of James Norris, who was reportedly good friends with his roommate. Forensics suggest that the body may have been dismembered, as evidence-"

I hardly heard the rest. I knew what the evidence would suggest, what the evidence *proved*.

They were back. For good, it seemed, no longer content to haunt us from the sidelines and watch us unravel.

Elsie let out a faint cry.

"My baby! You'll eat my baby!"

She cast a fearful finger in my direction, as though she were able to pierce and pin me to the sofa, before she ran out of the room, the throw a crumpled mess on Laura's chestnut floor.

"- youngest son of gaming tycoon Leonard Walburgess. The Frenchman, renowned for having founded the popular board game 'Invaders' and its role-playing counterpart 'The Incoming', gave a statement earlier this year denouncing his family's involvement in the tragic event that took place in his family home-"

I faintly became aware of my chest heaving panicked breaths and the now familiar sound of a door slamming, Laura and Dean's voices rising as they neared the room.

"-Didn't I say it would? Monsters, the lot-"

"-can't keep blaming *children* for what happened-"

"-destroyed everything since he got here-"

"-please! The cracks were there-"

Hanna's hand found mine.

I could only stare down at our mingled hands.

Keep your eyes on your post, Hanna.

"- notorious feud over the game's ownership had continued for almost a decade, until the death of Susan Lane in an apparent suicide nine years ago, caused the three families to seemingly reconcile. Since his son's death, Mr Lane has not been heard from, however sources suggest-"

As the room grew louder, I heard nothing else, my every nerve locked in at the feel of her hand, all the while oblivious as the monsters slowly invaded the house.

Incoming.

When the dust settled, the croaking sound of gnawing bones come to an end, no one dared move as the hulking beasts clawed their way out from the bloodbath, and out into the wailing storm.

As the shock wore off, the horror, regret, and wealth of self-loathing began to mount, tangible against the fine scarlet mist of the red-eyed-storm, but it came too late.

Much too late.

I swallowed, thickly, and waited as the first of the inevitable tears began to fall, carving deep, bloodied welts.

Soft footsteps filled the silence of the room, tentative with the hesitation of one afraid to approach the shadows that lurk beneath the bed.

Much too late.

Elsie's piercing screams tore the frail stillness of room apart, and as the first of many acrid notes joined her wails, I squeezed the hand still in mine, and resolutely kept my gaze to the crimson spattered floor, ignoring everyone else.

Just you and me.

And Them.

They'd come to learn what it meant to survive.

EPILOGUE

Elsie gave birth a few months later. A girl.

She named her Hanna.

The Incoming

A small town is shaken after the gruesome
death of twelve-year-old Harrison Lane.
The suspects- his four closest friends.

No one believes them when they blame it on
the monsters, yet as strange happenings
follow them to their new homes, they are
forced to confront the truth, else risk
destroying everyone around them.

Incoming. (2024)

Richard Keanes has only his mother and his
friends in his life. Yet when a seemingly
freak occurrence costs him everything and
everyone he cares about, he is forced to face
the aftermath alone- and the end is only the
beginning.

Incoming: Road Runner (2024) *

Matthieu Walburgess had everything- until
That Night. Sent to Father John's Guided

Academy, a Catholic reformation school, Matthieu tries to make the most of what he's left with, while shadows from his past appear, determined to destroy his one chance at redemption.

Incoming: Red Light (2024) *

Dennis St. Louis was already on his second chance when the monsters appeared. Now he's in a country he barely remembers, with a man he's never met and an impending sense of dread. While everyone tries to forget, Dennis is plagued by the memories, which he seems to remember clearer than anyone else.

When tragedy strikes again, Dennis risks it all to make things right.

Incoming: Shadows of a Lion's Claw (2025) *

Xzalia Naidoo has lived by the tales of her warrior ancestors her entire life, determined to follow in their footsteps. As Commander, she was labelled the mastermind in a night of horrors she was unable to prevent and is taken back to her homeland, where she learns the truth of what it means to be a leader- when things go wrong, it's you who pays the ultimate price.

Printed in Great Britain
by Amazon

45067449R00030